SCARLETT AND SAM

WHALE OF A TALE

by Eric A. Kimmel

illustrations by Ivica Stevanovic

KAR-BEN
PUBLISHING

KAR-BEN PUBLISHING
A division of Lerner Publishing Group, Inc.
241 First Avenue North
Minneapolis, MN 55401 USA
1-800-4-Karben

Website address: www.karben.com

Additional image credits: Dimitris66/Getty Images (sea foam);
Savushkin/Getty Images (old paper).

Main body text set in Janson Text LT Std 13/20.
Typeface provided by Adobe Systems.

Library of Congress Cataloging-in-Publication Data

Names: Kimmel, Eric A., author | Stevanovic, Ivica, illustrator.
Title: Whale of a tale / by Eric A. Kimmel ; illustrated by Ivica Stevanovic.
Description: Minneapolis : Kar-Ben Publishing, [2019] | Series: [Scarlett
    and Sam] | Summary: Scarlett and Sam go back to ancient Israel, where
    they find themselves on a ship with Jonah, who is determined not to be a
    prophet.
Identifiers: LCCN 2018033354 | ISBN 9781541522169 (lb : alk. paper) | ISBN
    9781541522176 (pb : alk. paper)
Subjects: | CYAC: Time travel—Fiction. | Jonah (Biblical prophet)—Fiction. |
    Brothers and sisters—Fiction. | Twins—Fiction. | Jaffa (Tel Aviv, Israel)—
    Fiction. | Nineveh (Extinct city)—Fiction. | Bible Old Testament—History
    of Biblical events—Fiction.
Classification: LCC PZ7.K5648 Wg 2019 | DDC [Fic]—dc23

LC record available at https://lccn.loc.gov/2018033354

PJ Library Edition ISBN 978-1-5415-8504-1

Manufactured in China
1-47379-48000-3/20/2019

091930.3K1/B1450/A8

CONTENTS

CHAPTER 1
CHECKMATE

Scarlett nudged a pawn one space across the chessboard. She sat back with a big grin on her face. "Now you're in trouble," she told Sam.

"Where?" Sam didn't believe her.

"Take a look. The bishop."

"No!" Sam exclaimed. "No! That's not fair! I didn't see that coming."

"That's what chess is about," Scarlett told him. "I believe you're finished. Checkmate."

Grandma Mina bustled around the kitchen, shuffling pots and pans between the stove and the oven. As usual, she had several dishes going at the same time. She glanced over at the kitchen table where Scarlett and Sam sat. "Checkmate, eh? Do you know where that comes from? It's Farsi. From Iran. *Shah mat!* It means 'the king is lost.' Helpless. Abandoned. That's what it means."

Sam studied the board. "My king's not finished yet," he told Scarlett. But if there was a way of saving him, Sam couldn't see it.

"Wasn't chess invented in India?" Scarlett asked Grandma Mina.

"No. It was invented in Iran!" Grandma Mina's family had lived happily in Iran for many years until a new government began to persecute the Jewish community, forcing Grandma Mina's family to leave. She was very proud of her Iranian heritage and considered herself very much an Iranian.

"Want me to reset the board?" Scarlett asked Sam. "We can have another game."

"No! I'm not done yet." He searched the board, looking for a solution that just wasn't there. That's when the telephone rang.

"One of you please get it! I have my hands full in here," Grandma Mina called from the stove. Scarlett picked up the phone. She listened.

"It's Mr. Dihanian from the carpet shop. He wants to know where you are," she called across the kitchen to Grandma Mina.

"Ay! I was supposed to bring the carpet down to his shop this morning to have it cleaned! I forgot!" Grandma Mina wailed. "I can't go now. I'm getting dinner ready."

"No problem," Sam said, still studying ways of eliminating that deadly pawn. "Tell him Grandma will bring it next week."

"Can she bring it down next week?" Scarlett asked Mr. Dihanian. She listened, then turned to

Grandma Mina. "Mr. Dihanian says he's leaving for Istanbul on a buying trip. If you can get the carpet to him today he might be able to work on it over the weekend and get it back to you before he goes. Otherwise, you'll have to wait till he gets back. That might be in a couple of months."

"I'm stuck," Sam finally admitted. "I guess it really is checkmate." He pushed over his king.

"I'm stuck too. *Shah mat* for me as well," said Grandma Mina.

"Maybe not," said Scarlett. "Why can't Sam and I bring the carpet to Mr. Dihanian for you?"

Grandma Mina laughed. "How are you going to get it there? You're not taking my carpet on the bus!" That carpet was the most precious treasure Grandma Mina owned. It had been in her family for centuries. The carpet was said to have magical powers. That may well have been true. The ayatollah's police in Iran had confiscated everything the family owned.

They even made Grandma Mina hand over her wedding ring. But for some strange reason they had left the carpet alone. As Grandma Mina told the story, it was as if they didn't see it, as if the carpet was invisible.

"We won't go on the bus. We'll take a car service," said Sam.

"What's a car service?" Grandma Mina asked as she stirred the soup.

"It just started in town a month ago. It's called Loft," said Sam. "It's an app on your cell phone. You open the app and enter where you want to go. Mom and Dad use the service. They let us put the app on our phones in case of an emergency. If we need to get home and they can't pick us up, we open the app and call a car," said Scarlett.

Grandma Mina shook her head. "Cars come out of the air. You pay for them out of the air. People used to say that the stories in the *Iranian Nights* were fantastic. No more fantastic than what's going on today. Who needs a lamp and a genie when you have happs and a cell phone?"

"Apps, Grandma. No *h*," said Scarlett.

"What are the *Iranian Nights*?" Sam asked.

"I think she means *Arabian Nights*."

"Tell Mr. Dihanian I'm sending you two down to him right now with the carpet. How long do you think it will take? You have to be back in time for dinner."

Scarlett spoke into the phone, relaying the message to Mr. Dihanian. "Sam and I are bringing the carpet now."

She hung up the phone and turned back to Grandma Mina. "It won't take us long. Maybe about an hour."

"Probably less. We'll drop off the carpet and have the car bring us right home," said Sam. He and Scarlett took the carpet down from the wall and carefully rolled it up. Scarlett and Sam were always glad to help Grandma Mina. Despite what Grandma Mina thought, dropping off her carpet at Mr. Dihanian's was no big deal. They were happy to help.

How long could it take?

CHAPTER 2
DOWNTOWN

Contrary to what Grandma Mina expected, the young man who came to pick up Scarlett and Sam looked completely ordinary. Red flannel shirt, jeans, close-cropped hair, and a beard.

He was polite, friendly, and helpful. He knew where Dihanian's carpet shop was. "Across the street from the library, right?" He opened the back of his red car and helped Scarlett and Sam put the carpet inside.

Grandma Mina fluttered around like a mother robin guarding her nest. "There's nothing that could stain my carpet? You don't carry any paint back here. Motor oil? Grease?"

"No, ma'am." The young man assured Grandma Mina that his car had recently been cleaned inside and out. He didn't transport paint, motor oil, body fluids, or nuclear waste. Satisfied, Grandma Mina switched to directing how the carpet should be put into the car.

"Careful now. That's it. This carpet's very old and very delicate. It can't handle rough treatment. Neither can I."

Scarlett, Sam, and the driver carefully eased the carpet into the back of the car as if they were placing a critically injured person into the back of an ambulance. They did have to lay it out at a diagonal and lift it up at the ends to make it fit, but not enough to upset Grandma Mina. She watched every step of the operation, finally nodding her approval when the carpet was safely inside.

"Be careful closing the back door!" she said. The young man knew better than to slam the hatchback down. He lowered it slowly, making sure no end of the carpet was caught as he pressed it down. The latch clicked into place.

Scarlett and Sam piled into the back seat.

"Be back before five," Grandma Mina said.

"We'll be back before three," Scarlett assured her. Meanwhile, Sam introduced himself to the driver.

"I'm Sam."

"Hi, I'm Jon," the driver said as he pulled out of the driveway.

"Short for Jonathan?"

"Not exactly. Short for Jonah."

"Have you been driving for Loft long?"

"Not too long."

"What did you do before?" Scarlett asked.

"That's a long story," Jon said.

"What?"

"It's like this . . ." Jon talked as he drove. He was a careful driver, stopping at red lights and stop signs, observing the speed limit, and signaling when changing lanes. They were soon on the freeway, heading for the bridge and downtown. "I had this job that I really loved. Really, really loved. Then one day my boss asked me to do something that I just couldn't do."

"Something illegal?" Sam asked.

"Nope. Nothing like that," said Jon. "In fact, most people would say it was something good. But not for me. I just couldn't do it. So I did the only thing I could do."

"What was that?" Scarlett asked. "You quit?"

"No," said Jon. "I wish I could have quit. That wasn't one of the options in my line of work. I ran away. I'm sure the boss is looking for me right now. He'll find me one day. I know that."

"Then what?" asked Sam.

Jon shrugged. "Who knows? He'll try to make

me do what he wants me to do. He'll make it rough for me if I don't. I don't care. Like I told him before, I'm not doing it. That's final."

"Gosh," said Sam. His curiosity was thoroughly aroused. "Are you sure you can't even give us a hint?"

"Nope," said Jon. "And do me a favor. After I drop you off, forget you ever met me. It will be better for all of us."

"Why?" Scarlett asked.

"Never mind," Jon said. "We're here."

***

Traffic was blocked on the street next to Dihanian's carpet shop. A truck driver was delivering crates of soft drinks to the Mexican restaurant on the corner. Jonah asked Scarlett and Sam if it would be okay for him to drop them off by the library since it was going to be hard for him to find a place to pull over.

"I really don't want to hang around here too long," he said. "You never know who's watching."

"I get it," said Sam, although neither he nor Scarlett really got it at all. Sam and Scarlett got out of the car. Sam shut the door. He and Scarlett waved goodbye to Jon as he drove off through the traffic.

"That was weird," Scarlett said.

"I wonder what his boss wanted him to do." Sam tried to imagine what it might be, but couldn't come up with anything that wasn't right out of an action movie. He and Scarlett crossed the street to Mr. Dihanian's shop.

"Hi, Mr. Dihanian!" Scarlett said as they came through the door.

Mr. Dihanian stared at them. "Where's the carpet?"

The full horror hit them. It was still in the back of the car. Talking about Jon's mysterious troubles had caused them to completely forget why they had come downtown in the first place.

"YAAAAAHHHHH!!!"

Scarlett and Sam ran out of the shop, tearing down the sidewalk, hoping to catch a glimpse of the red car.

"There it is!" Sam yelled. But when they got close, they saw a blonde woman at the wheel.

Where could he have gone? Scarlett asked herself.

"He could have gone anywhere. Maybe we can contact Loft and find out," said Sam.

"How?" said Scarlett.

Sam fumbled with his cell phone. "The app's up. They have a 'contact' button. Should I try it?"

"Sure. Answer a bunch of questions, and someone will get back to you tomorrow. Maybe. We don't have time for that, Sam. We have to find that carpet, or Grandma Mina will serve US up for dinner." Scarlett looked up and down the street. A red car suddenly made a U-turn.

Scarlett grabbed Sam's arm. "Could that be him?"

"Maybe," said Sam. "He's got the turn signal on. We've got nothing to lose. Let's head him off."

Scarlett and Sam ran into the middle of the street, waving their arms.

"Stop! STOP!"

Cars swerved to avoid them. Horns blared. Drivers leaned out their windows to yell. A tour bus came barreling down at them. They saw the driver talking with the tourists. Didn't he see them in the street? It didn't look as if the bus was going to slow down.

"Scarlett!" yelled Sam.

"Sam!" yelled Scarlett.

And then . . .

CHAPTER 3
CARPETS FOR SALE

"Get out of the way? What's the matter with you? You're blocking the road!"

Scarlett and Sam, huddled together, opened their eyes. They were still in the middle of the road, but it was like no road they had ever seen before. It wasn't paved, just covered with dust and dirt. And while there was plenty of traffic, there wasn't a motor vehicle in sight. There were plenty of mules, donkeys, and people walking around without paying too much attention to traffic lights and stop signs—mostly because there weren't any.

"Are you going to get out of the way, or are we going to stand here all day, staring at each other?" There went that angry voice again. Sam looked up and found himself staring into the broad face of an ox.

"I didn't know an ox could talk!" said Sam.

"They don't. It's that guy." Scarlett pointed to the man standing beside a cart that an ox was pulling. He had a long, black beard and an odd-looking felt cap on his head. He wore something that looked like a long T-shirt that came down to his knees, belted in the middle. On his feet were rough-looking sandals laced up with string.

"Well?" the man demanded.

"We're moving. We're moving," said Scarlett, pulling a still-bewildered Sam out of the way.

The ox let out a snort. The cart moved on with the man grumbling all the while, ". . . just stand in the middle of the street . . . block traffic . . . you think everybody has all day . . . nobody's in a hurry . . .".

Scarlett and Sam found a quiet corner under an awning next to a man selling dates.

"Want to buy some dates?" he asked them.

"No, thanks," Scarlett said.

"I'll make you a good deal. Two minas for twenty shekels."

"No, thanks," said Sam.

"A camel load came in yesterday from Palmyra. They're really good. You won't find sweeter dates in all of Jaffa."

"Jaffa? Is that where we are?" Scarlett asked. She and Sam knew enough about Israel to recognize the name of the main seaport.

"Where else? If we were in Tyre or Zidon, we'd be speaking Phoenician. Not that it's much different from Hebrew. The Phoenicians have been good friends and allies for many, many years, since the days of King Solomon."

Scarlett and Sam looked at each other. From the way the date seller spoke, King Solomon must have lived a long time ago.

"Solomon was a great and wise king," said Sam. "He made Israel a great nation."

"We could sure use him now." A woman selling pita bread out of a basket joined the conversation.

"Israel isn't doing well?" Scarlett asked. The date seller and the pita seller both laughed.

"Not doing well? It doesn't even exist. There is no Israel."

"What do you mean," Sam asked.

"Where are you two from? Don't you know any history?" the pita seller asked. "The people in the north couldn't get along with the people in the south. So they set up their own country: Israel. It didn't do them any good. They still fought and quarreled with each other and all of their neighbors. Finally, the Assyrians came along. They flattened the land and took everyone as slaves. There is no more Israel. The rest of us are barely holding on."

"Who are the Assyrians?" Sam asked.

"Imagine all the plagues of Egypt rolled together," the pita seller told him. "There was still an Egypt, even after the plagues passed through the land. But the Assyrians leave nothing behind. Israel was once a prosperous country. Now it's a wasteland. And they'll be back."

Scarlett felt her stomach begin to hurt. "If Israel is gone, this is . . ."

"Judea. That's what we call ourselves now," said the date seller.

"And your king is . . . ?" Sam asked.

"Ahaz," the pita seller told him. "You don't want to tangle with him. He may be Solomon's descendant, but he sure isn't wise."

"Or good," the date seller added.

***

Scarlett and Sam spent the next few hours walking aimlessly around the winding streets and alleys of Jaffa, trying to absorb what they had just learned. They both came to the same conclusion.

"This isn't a pleasant place or time. We need to get out of here," said Sam.

"How?" Scarlett asked. "We've lost Grandma Mina's carpet. And Grandma Mina says it's magic. It could help us get back home. How are we going to get it back? We may not even be in the same century. What if we're stuck in ancient Jaffa and the carpet is driving around town in the back of a red car?"

"Maybe we can find another carpet," Sam suggested.

"And pay for it with what? And how will we get it back home?"

Sam shrugged. "Got a better idea?"

"No."

"Then let's start looking. Who knows? We might get lucky."

***

They hadn't gone far when they ran into a man carrying a pile of ratty-looking blankets over his shoulder.

"Where did you get those?" Scarlett asked him.

"At the *shuk*." The man pointed down the street.

"What's a *shuk*?" Sam asked.

"Market. Big market," the man exclaimed as he scurried down an alley.

He wasn't exaggerating. The *shuk* was easily the biggest building in Jaffa. The main *shuk* was a two-story mud brick building that went on for blocks. Around it was a cluster of awnings, tents, and open-air booths selling anything that could be sold.

Shopkeepers' eager hands clutched at Scarlett and Sam as they pushed their way through the crowds of shoppers.

"Goat cheese! The best!"

"Hummus! Buy my hummus!"

"Singing birds from Lebanon!"

"Rare wine from Greece. Care for a sip, young sir or madam?"

"No, thanks," Scarlett and Sam said over and over again. They finally reached the entrance to the main building. A sleepy, old man with a long beard looked them over.

"We're looking to buy a carpet. Where can we find one?" Sam asked the man.

The man yawned. "Street of the Carpet Sellers. Many carpets. Many sellers."

Sam didn't understand what the man was talking about until he saw how the *shuk* was laid out. The market was divided into different sections like a department store. Unlike the chaos and confusion in the booth section outside, the merchants in here had their own spaces based on what they were selling. If you wanted pots and pans, you went to one area. If you wanted hats, you went to another. If you wanted carpets . . .

"Sort of like a department store at the mall. Only without an elevator," said Scarlett.

"Or a movie theater," Sam added. "Or a parking lot."

"I see the carpet sellers," said Scarlett, counting off the aisles. "We're almost there."

The aisle of the carpet sellers was impossible to miss. Heaps of carpets bursting with bright colors and intricate designs filled the stalls. Suddenly Scarlett grasped Sam's shoulder.

"Hey! Do you see what I see? Isn't that Grandma Mina's carpet?"

"It sure looks like it," said Sam. "How did it get here?"

"How did we get here?" said Scarlett. "Who knows? But if we can get the carpet back and if we can get it to work its magic, maybe we won't have to be here much longer."

One of the carpet sellers smoothed out Grandma Mina's carpet as he added it to the pile in front of his booth. Sam ran to grab it.

"Hey! Hands off!" The carpet seller yanked Sam by the shoulders and shoved him away. "These are valuable items. Genuine handwoven rugs from Medea and Persia. They need to be handled with care. Don't touch the carpet unless you mean to buy it."

"We don't have to buy it. It's not your carpet. It's ours!" Scarlett said.

"Nonsense," the carpet seller told her. "I just bought it from a man an hour ago. He said he needed to sell it to pay for passage on a ship leaving Jaffa today."

"Where was he going?" Sam asked.

The carpet seller shrugged. "How should I know? I buy carpets. I don't ask questions."

"That man had no right to sell it. That carpet's ours," Sam insisted.

"But we're not going to argue with you," said Scarlett. "We need that carpet, and we need it bad. How much do you want for it?"

The carpet seller rubbed his beard. "People will say I'm crazy, but I'll let you have this beautiful rug for . . . what do you say . . . 20,000 shekels?"

"How much is that in our money?" Scarlett whispered to Sam.

"I don't know," Sam said. "It may not matter. How much have you got?"

Scarlett dug in her pockets. "$5.50."

"I have $10 and a little change," Sam said.

"Something tells me that 20,000 shekels is more than that." Scarlett turned to the carpet seller. "Will you take $15.85?"

"15,850 shekels? Make it an even 16,000 and we have a deal."

"Um . . . not exactly," said Scarlett.

"Then you'll get nothing." Sam grabbed for the carpet, but not fast enough. The carpet seller jerked it out of his hands. "Thieves! Help! Call the *Shomrim*!"

Shuk Security—otherwise known as the *Shomrim*—came storming down the aisles from all directions. One look told Scarlett and Sam that these guys were not friendly mall cops who would tell you to behave and give you a warning. These *Shomrim* looked pretty fierce.

"Forget the carpet. We need to leave. NOW!" said Scarlett.

***

Leave they did. As fast as they could. Right through the middle of the *shuk*, knocking over trays, carts, food, displays, and anything or anyone in their way. That slowed down the *Shomrim*, who had to shove their way through screaming shoppers, enraged merchants, and heaps of spilled merchandise.

"Which way?" Sam shouted to Scarlett as they scurried past the bearded man at the entrance.

"Whichever way looks good," she shouted back. They ducked into a narrow alley, following its twists and turns to an open plaza where the tall masts of ships pierced the cloudless sky. They smelled the ocean. They heard gulls crying overhead and waves lapping against the shore.

"We're at the sea!" Scarlett shouted. She glanced over her shoulder to see if the *Shomrim* were still following them.

"Better run! They're after you!" several sailors called to them from a ship that was pulling away from the dock. The *Shomrim* came running across the plaza. "There they are!" they yelled, dashing after Scarlett and Sam.

"Jump!" the sailors cried. Scarlett and Sam ran to the edge of the pier and leapt aboard. The *Shomrim* stood at the edge of the dock, shaking their fists at the sailors and shouting, "Those two are shoplifters! Bring them back, or we'll report you to King Ahaz!"

The captain stood at the rudder with his hand cupped to his ear. "Sorry, guys! Can't hear you!" he called to the *Shomrim* onshore. The wind filled the sails as the ship sailed out of the harbor and onto the open sea.

CHAPTER 4

ROW, ROW, ROW YOUR BOAT

As soon as the ship was underway, the captain turned the rudder over to the mate and sat down on a coil of rope to talk with Scarlett and Sam. He wrapped his arms around his knees and asked, "So! What brings you two here?"

Scarlett and Sam looked at each other. Where to begin? And how much to tell without making the captain and crew think they were making things up. Scarlett spoke first.

"Our grandmother has this carpet . . ."

"It brought us to the *shuk* . . ." Sam added.

"So you brought your poor grandma's carpet to the *shuk* to sell. That was your first mistake," the captain said. "I wouldn't go near that place. Not anymore. Not since Ahaz became king."

"Why not?" Scarlett asked.

"We used to bring our goods into Jaffa and sell them on the dock," the captain said. "But no more. The *Shomrim* say we must buy and sell everything only in the *shuk*. Merchants must pay the king a rental fee for their booths. Add on the special fees and taxes, and it's hardly worth it for us to come into Jaffa's port anymore. Usually we just continue up the coast to Tyre, where the Phoenicians treat us fairly."

"We didn't know that," said Scarlett.

"And we didn't have any choice in coming to Jaffa," Sam added.

"Well, better luck next time." The captain continued what he thought was their story, as the walls and towers of Jaffa sank below the horizon. "So, you offered your grandma's carpet to the rug sellers and they offered you beans? When you refused their offer, they kept the carpet." The captain shook his head. "It's an old tale. I tell my crew to watch out for those sharks whenever we're in port. They'll gobble you up faster than the sharks at sea. But, don't you worry. You're safe now."

"Thanks," Scarlett said. "You can let us off somewhere along the coast. We can find our way back home."

"Sorry," the captain said. "We're not stopping along the coast. We're heading west."

"How far west?" Sam asked.

"As far west as you can go," the captain told him. "We'll make stops along the way at Knossos, Mycenae, and Carthage, and we end our voyage in Tarshish."

"Where's that?" Sam asked the captain.

"In Hispania," answered the captain, standing up. "Talk to you later. I hear the mate calling. We have to trim the jib."

"What's a jib?" Scarlett asked as the captain left.

"What's Hispania?" asked Sam.

"I think he means Spain," Scarlett told him. "We studied it in history class at school when we learned about explorers to the new world."

"Well!" exclaimed Sam. "We just left Jaffa. That means this ship is heading . . . for the other end of the Mediterranean Sea!"

That thought knocked them both for a loop. How would they get back home if they were on the other side of the ocean from Grandma Mina's carpet? Maybe it would turn up on its own; it was magic after all. But Scarlett and Sam weren't so sure. The carpet would need GPS just to find them. And what were they supposed to do in Spain while they waited for the carpet to show up?

If it even ever showed up. That was a disturbing thought. They'd be totally on their own. For months. For years. Maybe forever!

"It might not be so bad. I like burritos," said Sam.

"Burritos come from Mexico not Spain," Scarlett reminded him. "Spanish people won't get to Mexico for another two thousand years."

Sam sighed. "That's a long time to wait for a burrito. How about a taco salad?"

***

They soon learned that finding a burrito was the least of their worries. The captain came back with a small matter to discuss with them.

"About your fare . . ."

"Fare?" said Scarlett.

"Yes," the captain said. "Our ship doesn't carry passengers for free. If you plan to travel with us as far as Hispania, there's going to be a slight charge."

"How slight?" Sam asked.

"That depends," said the captain. "We have different plans. We can offer you either first class, business, or coach."

"How much is coach?" Scarlett asked. Grandma Mina always told them how much prices had gone up over the years. Since they were about twenty-five hundred years back in history now, maybe they could get a Mediterranean cruise for the fifteen dollars they had between them. Sam held out the crumpled bills.

"Will this cover it?"

The captain blinked. "Is that some kind of parchment?"

"You could say that. It's very rare," Sam told him. He showed the captain the portraits of Abraham Lincoln and Alexander Hamilton on the two bills. "These are famous people where Scarlett and I come from." He didn't say that they wouldn't become famous for a couple of thousand years.

The captain did not look impressed. "Don't you have any gold or silver?"

"No."

"Jewels? Silk? Goods to trade? Anything?"

"Afraid not," said Sam.

"All we had was Grandma Mina's carpet. Those merchants in the *shuk* took it from us," Scarlett said.

The captain sighed. "I suppose I could sell you in the slave market when we stop off in Egypt."

"NO!" Scarlett and Sam shouted. Being slaves in Egypt was an experience they had read about at many Passover seders.

"Relax. Just kidding," the captain said. "I wouldn't do that. I wouldn't sell anybody as a slave. Some captains do. They'll carry only what they can sell. But I think slavery is a different story. I don't care how much money I could make. It's an ugly business, and I want no part of it. We do have another option that might suit you. It's our travel/work study plan."

"What's that?" asked Scarlett.

The captain explained. "You travel with the rest of the passengers and crew, learning about the people, the cultures, and the customs of the different places where we'll be stopping. It's just that you'll be expected to pitch in from time to time when we need extra hands."

"That sounds fair," said Sam. "We'll take it. What sort of work would you like us to do?"

The captain glanced up at the slackening sail. The wind had died down. "As a matter of fact," he said, "I can show you right now."

***

"Travel/work study, eh?" Scarlett grumbled as she pulled back on the oar. She sat beside Sam as they and the other sailors rowed the ship through the waves.

"Keep together. Follow the beat," the mate called

to rowers as he pounded out the rhythm on a drum. *BOOM*—stroke! *BOOM*—stroke!

"Does this remind you of anything?" Sam asked Scarlett.

"Yeah, that old movie *Ben Hur* that Grandma Mina likes to watch. At least some guy isn't beating us with a whip like they did aboard that Roman ship in the movie," Scarlett answered.

"Let's speed it up," the captain said, dropping by to see how they were doing. "I want to go waterskiing."

Scarlett nearly dropped her oar.

"Ha, ha!" the captain laughed. "Just kidding. Keep it up. You kids are doing fine. Rowing is great exercise. You'll have terrific abs by the time we get to Hispania. This is how it is when we sail the Great Sea. Sometimes you sail; sometimes you row. It all depends on the wind."

"How much longer do we have to row? I'm getting tired," said Sam.

"Another hour. Then we'll take a break," the captain said. "Keep at it. You guys are awesome."

"Yeah, right!" Scarlett grumbled. "We're having such a wonderful time. It's almost like being on vacation." Between the creak of the oars and the beat of the drum, she almost didn't hear Sam whispering.

"Scarlett . . . *psst*, Scarlett!"

"What?" She was in no mood for conversation.

"Look over there. On the other side of the ship. What do they call it . . . starboard? Fifth bench from the bow. I think we know that guy. Isn't he . . ."

Scarlett nearly dropped her oar. "The guy from the Loft car who dropped us off downtown! If that's not him, it's somebody who looks just like him. How can that be? If it's the same guy, what's he doing here?"

"Quiet down," the mate called. "More effort. Less chatter. Let's go, everybody! Keep together!" *BOOM*—stroke! *BOOM*—stroke!"

***

They rowed for another hour. Then the wind
came up. The mate told them they could stop
rowing and stack their oars in a special rack. By
then, most of the rowers were so tired they could
hardly lift their oars to stack them. Not Scarlett
and Sam. They discovered new energy now that
they had business to complete.

They both kept their eyes on the man as he
stacked his oar, and then squatted on the deck for a
snack of bread and dates. Scarlett and Sam walked
over and sat down on either side of him.

"Hi, Jon! Remember us? How are the dates?"
Scarlett asked.

The man stared at her. "Do I know you?"

"Maybe you forgot," Scarlett answered. "But we
didn't."

"Red car . . . Loft . . . downtown . . . Dihanian's
carpet shop. Any of that ring a bell?" asked Sam.

"Leave me alone. I don't know what you're talking about." The man tried to get up. Scarlett and Sam pulled him down.

"We think you do," Scarlett said. "We can't explain everything that's going on, but we can promise you one thing. We're not going to leave you alone until you start talking. We're on a ship. There's nowhere to go but overboard, so don't think about skipping out on us."

"We don't want to cause you any trouble, Jon," said Sam. "Just talk to us. Why are you here? You look scared. You told us you were running from your boss. Tell us why. Maybe we can help you."

"We're good at helping," Scarlett added.

The young man looked around the deck to see if anyone else was listening. "All right," he said. "I'll tell you. But you have to promise not to breathe a word of what I say to anyone. I'm in trouble. Big trouble. But no one can help me. Especially not two kids."

"Are you sure?"

"Oh, I'm sure," he said. "Let's start at the beginning. They call me Jon, but my name is Jonah. And I'm not a Loft driver. I'm a prophet."

Scarlett's eyes opened wide. She was beginning to get the picture.

CHAPTER 5

JONAH'S STORY

The twins listened as Jonah began his story.

Jonah

It wasn't my idea to be a prophet. I wanted to be a farmer, like my dad, Amitai. I'm good at making things grow.

It was getting close to Sukkot. I was in back of the house, sorting out the different boards and poles we use to build the sukkah. It was a bright, sunny day. Nothing out of the ordinary. Suddenly I heard a voice out of the sky.

"JONAH!"

Did somebody call me? I looked around. I thought maybe it was my dad. I couldn't see anyone in the backyard, so I went back to what I was doing. That's when I heard the voice again. Only louder this time. Lots louder, like a clap of thunder.

"JONAH!!!"

I stopped working on the sukkah. "You don't have to yell," I told whoever it was. "I can hear you. What do you want?"

The voice spoke again. "I want you."

"Me? What for? Look, I'm busy. I'm trying to get ready for Sukkot. Who are you anyway? Where are you hiding?"

"I am not hiding. You cannot see Me, but I am all around you, closer to you than your heartbeat. I am everywhere. Who am I? I am Who I am."

That's when I began to get scared. I'd heard those words before. That's what God said to Moses from the burning bush. I knew then that I was hearing the voice of God.

God's the Big Boss, the biggest in the universe. And when the Big Boss talks, you listen. I began trembling. What would God want me to do? Would he ask me to sacrifice my son, like Abraham was asked to sacrifice his son Isaac? I was off the hook for that one. I didn't have any kids. Would he send me to Pharaoh in Egypt to tell him to let my people go? No worries there. We left Egypt generations ago. So what exactly did God want me to do?

Had I known, I would have bought my ticket for Egypt that afternoon. If I had ten kids, I would have sacrificed them all. Because what God wanted from me was a hundred times scarier than anything I could imagine.

God said, "Get up, Jonah! I need you to do something important. I need you to do it right now."

"What?" I asked, trembling.

"Go to Nineveh, that great city. Preach to the people there. Tell them I've had enough of their wickedness and evil deeds. Warn them to change their ways or My anger will fall on them."

"Who, me?" I said.

"Yes, you!" God answered. "Leave now. You have a long journey ahead."

***

I left that afternoon. I had a long journey—but not to Nineveh. No way was I going there!

Nineveh is the capital of Assyria. It's a terrible place. The Assyrians are evil. When they conquer a country, they leave nothing behind. After they conquered Samaria, the capital of Israel, there wasn't one stone standing on another. They marched the few remaining survivors off as slaves. The whole land was nothing but a valley of dry bones.

I wanted nothing to do with Nineveh or Assyrians. I wasn't going to preach to them. I didn't want God to forgive them. If God was just, the Assyrians would be punished, not given a chance to change their ways.

But how do you say no to God, the Biggest Boss of all? I just wanted God to be fair and to punish those Assyrians, not allow them to repent and be forgiven. I didn't know what to do, so I hid in a cave. I don't remember how long I was there. It's hard to keep track of days when you can't see the sun. When I came out of that cave, I found myself in a different place. Very different!

It was amazing! There were wagons that ran by themselves without horses or donkeys to pull them. There were hundreds of people scurrying about, not looking at anything except little devices that they carried in their hands. They talked to the devices. They poked them. I tried to talk to the people, but no one could hear me. Everyone had these strings from their devices stuck in their ears. It was all very strange.

But I figured I could hide out there. Nobody would find me if I could find a way to fit in. So I got clothes at a shuk called Goodwill. I made friends who taught me how to drive those horseless vehicles called cars. I began driving for Loft. Life was good, even though the place was very strange and not at all like my home. I had a place to live. I figured that no one—not even the Big Boss—could find me.

Was I ever wrong! As soon as I dropped you off near the carpet store, I heard the voice again.

"JONAH! WHAT ARE YOU DOING THERE? I NEED YOU IN NINEVEH!"

"Okay, okay," I thought. I parked the car. I was desperate. Maybe somehow I could figure out how to get back to my cave. But I sure didn't want to go to Nineveh.

I found your carpet when I was getting my things

out of the back of the car. I didn't mean to keep it. I just didn't know how to get it back to you and I didn't have a lot of time, so I took it with me.

I closed my eyes and somehow, I found myself not in my cave but in Jaffa. That actually suited my plan perfectly. I ran down to the port and looked for the ship that was going farthest. When the captain told me he was bound for Tarshish, I sold the carpet. I know the guy in the *shuk* got it for much less than it was worth, but I got enough to pay my way to Hispania. I bought my ticket and boarded the ship. Tarshish is truly the end of the earth. You can't get farther from Nineveh than that.

***

"That's a good story," Sam said. "I'm just not sure whether or not I believe it. And we want our carpet back. Grandma Mina will be furious with us if we come back without it."

"You're not kidding," Scarlett added. She turned to Jonah. "I don't know whether I should believe you either. Closing your eyes and opening them in another time and place?"

Jonah shrugged. "Well that's what happened. You can believe it or not, as you wish. Right now it's time for dinner. All that rowing gave me an appetite. See you around." Jonah headed toward the gangway leading to the galley.

"What do you think?" Sam asked Scarlett.

"It could be the truth," Scarlett said. "After all, his story is no crazier than ours. If we can go back to Bible times, why can't someone from Bible times go forward to our time? What counts is Jonah doing what God told him to do. God told him to go to Nineveh. And he's not doing it."

"But he's scared of the Assyrians," said Sam. "And he doesn't think God is being fair. If even half of what Jonah told us about Assyria and Nineveh is true, I don't blame him."

"Well," said Scarlett. "Jonah thinks the Assyrians should not have treated their enemies—like Israel and all the other countries they conquered—so badly. Maybe he's afraid that if he preaches to them, they just might change their ways. Then God wouldn't destroy them."

"What's wrong with that?" Sam asked.

"Between you and me, nothing," said Scarlett. "But for Jonah, plenty. He wants to see the Assyrians punished for their wicked ways. He doesn't think God is being fair."

"What are we going to do?" Sam asked.

"We're going to get Jonah to go to Nineveh and deliver the message the Big Boss told him to deliver, whether he wants to or not."

"And then?"

"And then we'll find Grandma Mina's carpet and figure out a way to get home."

CHAPTER 6
STORMY WEATHER

Scarlett and Sam were talking about what to do next when they heard the captain shouting.

"All hands on deck! Batten down the hatches! Furl the sails! Passengers go below. We're in for some bad weather!"

"What's going on?" Scarlett and Sam asked him.

"No time to talk. Look over there." The captain pointed toward the horizon. Scarlett and Sam saw a thick band of black clouds approaching from the west. Bolts of lightning flashed. They heard thunder in the distance.

"This storm will be a big one," the captain said. "We don't have time to seek shelter. We're too far away from the nearest harbor. We'll have to ride it out at sea. Let's hope our ship holds together."

He hurried forward to direct the sailors. They had already furled the sail and were lowering the mast. "I'll take the rudder!" Scarlett and Sam heard the captain call to the first mate. "We may just make it if we can keep the bow heading into the wind. All passengers go below. Batten down the hatches."

"This is going to be bad," Sam said to Scarlett.

"I hope I don't get seasick," Scarlett replied. They gripped the rail to keep from blowing overboard by the rising wind. Sam had to shout so Scarlett could hear him. "We'd better do what the captain says and get below!"

Within moments, the full fury of the storm came sweeping down on them.

Lighting flashed. The ship's timbers vibrated with the crashing thunder. Scarlett struggled to keep her footing as huge waves washed over the deck. Sam grabbed her to keep her from being swept overboard. Inch by inch, Scarlett and Sam made their way across the deck to the hatchway, pulling the hatch shut behind them. But not soon enough. A torrent of seawater washed through the opening.

"You're soaked!" Scarlett exclaimed. "You'd better change before you catch cold."

"Change into what?" Sam asked. He was right. They hadn't exactly packed for this trip. Scarlett and Sam glanced around the hold. Passengers lay on sacks and boxes, too scared to move. Others, frightfully seasick, were lying facedown, vomiting. Bilge water sloshed over everybody as the ship rolled back and forth. The only light came from a tiny oil lamp hanging from the ceiling.

"Where's Jonah? Do you see him?" Scarlett asked.

Sam pointed to a form huddled on top of a stack of wine jars. "There he is! Fast asleep."

"How can he sleep through a storm like this? It's . . ." She never finished the sentence. At that moment, a huge crash of thunder rattled the ship. Its timbers groaned as if they might come apart at any moment. The passengers in the hold started crying and screaming.

"Help!"

"We're doomed!"

"We're going to drown!"

The hatch flew open. The captain shouted down into the hold, trying to make himself heard over the raging storm. "Get up on deck, all of you! The ship's breaking up! We're not going to make it! Now's the time to call on whatever god you worship! Only the gods can save us now!"

Scarlett and Sam struggled onto the deck with the rest of the passengers. The wind nearly blew them overboard as they emerged from the hatchway. Scarlett and Sam saw the sailors kneeling on deck, lifting their arms in prayer as the wind howled and the rain whipped their faces.

"Oh, Marduk! Have mercy on me!"

"Isis, spare my life!"

"Great Ishtar, hear my prayer!"

"Poseidon, ruler of the sea, save me from the wind and waves!"

Sam began his own prayer: "Ruler of the earth and sky, we call on You to have mercy on us and everyone aboard this ship. Protect us all from the storm. Shield us all from thunder and lightning. Shelter us all beneath Your wings, and guide us to a safe harbor. Amen."

"Hey, where's Jonah?" asked Scarlett suddenly. "Did he get swept overboard?"

"No," said Sam. "I don't think he ever came up on deck. I'll bet he's still asleep down in the hold."

Just then the captain lurched by, holding tight to the rail. His face was pale with fright in the lightning flashes. "Where's your friend?" he shouted at Scarlett and Sam.

"Down in the hold. I think he's still asleep," Sam shouted back.

"Asleep? How can anybody sleep through this? Wake him up, and get him up on deck if he wants to save himself! We're likely to capsize any moment if these waves don't shatter us first. We need every soul aboard to pray to their gods to help us. It's up to the gods now."

"I'll get him," Scarlett said. As she turned to go down into the hold, the hatch opened. Jonah climbed out. He looked like someone just awakened from a nap. He didn't seem surprised by the storm.

"What's all the noise?" he asked.

Scarlett and Sam stared at each other. What did he think was going on? They were obviously in the middle of a storm!

"Start praying to your gods," the captain shouted at him.

"It won't do any good," Jonah said. "God doesn't want your ship. God wants me. I am the reason God sent this storm."

"Tell your god to unsend it. Ask for your god's mercy before we all drown. How can we appease your god?" the captain said.

"You must throw me overboard," Jonah said to the captain. "That's really what God wants. If you throw me overboard, your ship will be saved."

"What?" The captain backed away, shaking his head. "No. No! I can't do that. I can't throw an innocent man into the sea. The gods would haunt me forever. Better for us all to be swallowed by the ocean than for me to perform such a wicked deed."

"Listen to me," Jonah told the captain. "You will all be swallowed by the ocean—you and everyone else aboard this ship—unless you do as I say. Save your ship. Save your crew. Throw me overboard."

The captain shook his head. Lightning lit up his face. Was it rain or tears streaming down his face?

"I could never do that. I'd rather drown."

"He won't do it," Scarlett told Jonah.

"Then the ship and crew will be lost," Jonah said. "They must throw me overboard. It's the only answer."

"You don't seem too concerned about drowning yourself," Sam said.

Jonah nodded. "It is what God wants. It is what God commands. I've told the captain what he must do."

Scarlett looked at Jonah. "Okay, Sam. Jonah says this is what God commands. So we know what we have to do."

"We do?" Sam answered.

"Yes. Grab his right hand. I'll take his left."

Scarlett and Sam pulled Jonah over to the ship's rail.

"You're going to Nineveh one way or another, Jonah. And we're going with you. Even if we all have to swim!" Scarlett said as she and Sam leapt overboard, taking Jonah with them.

The waves closed over their heads as the winds carried the ship onward.

CHAPTER 7
SHARK WEEK

The wind died down. The dark clouds scattered. The full moon came out. Its reflection shone over the sea.

Scarlett, Sam, and Jonah drifted along with the ocean currents until dawn. They were floating in a large wooden tub they'd found, drifting in a mat of storm debris that rose and fell with the waves. It was just big enough to hold the three of them as long as they didn't move around too much. The lip of the tub was barely six inches above the water.

"Looks like the storm has passed," Scarlett said, watching the red sun rise out of the sea. There was no land in sight. No ships, either, or anyone else clinging to wreckage. The twins wondered if the people on the ship had made it through the storm. They hoped so.

Aside from fish and seagulls, it seemed as if Scarlett, Jonah, and Sam were the only living souls in the vast ocean.

"Do you think that the captain might turn the ship around and come looking for us to see if we made it?" Scarlett tried to sound hopeful.

"I doubt it," Jonah said. But he didn't seem worried.

"Do you suppose there are sharks out here?" Sam asked. He had been watching a TV show about sharks the previous week, and they were very much on his mind. Sam liked sharks, and he knew a lot about them. But he also knew they were dangerous.

"There's an easy way to find out," Jonah said

with a grin. "Stick your hand in the water."

"Not funny," Scarlett snapped. "We're in this mess because of you. We ought to throw you into the water to test for sharks."

"But you won't. Because you and your brother are good people. You wouldn't do anything like that. But even if you did, nothing would happen. God wants me to go to Nineveh, and God's not going to let anything happen to me until I do."

"You sound like you really do know what's going to happen to us. What makes you so sure?" Sam asked.

Jonah shrugged his shoulders. "I'm a prophet."

"Why would God have made you a prophet?" Scarlett blurted out. "You don't seem like a prophet. You don't seem very courageous. You don't have a prophet license. It's just that, for some reason, God decided to make you a prophet. So please do us a favor and do what God wants you to do—go to Nineveh!"

Jonah sighed. "If we're given the choice, I prefer sharks to Assyrians. Also, I couldn't get to Nineveh if I wanted to."

"Why not?" Sam asked.

"Basic geography," Jonah explained. "Nineveh is on the Tigris River, which empties into the Gulf of Arabia. To get there from where we are now, in the middle of the Great Sea, we'd have to go to Hispania, sail through the Great Pillars, then go all the way around Africa. Nobody's ever done it. Or at least managed to come back and tell about it. It would be a huge undertaking even if we had a ship. And, in case you haven't noticed, all we've got is a leaky tub that isn't going to get us anywhere unless we start bailing."

"There has to be a way," Scarlett grumbled, as she, Sam, and Jonah began scooping up water with their hands and throwing it over the side.

Sam raised his head. "Did you just hear something?"

Scarlett and Jonah stopped bailing. "No," they said.

"Shhh! Be quiet for a minute and let me listen," Sam said. "There! I hear it again."

"Me too!" said Scarlett excitedly. "It sounds like some kind of music. DA-dum, DA-Dum, DA-Dum . . ."

"Now I hear it too and it's getting louder," Jonah said. "Weird—to hear music out here in the middle of the sea. What do you suppose it is?"

"I don't know," said Sam. "It reminds me of the soundtrack of that movie . . ."

"What movie?" Scarlett asked.

"You know! The one about the . . . SHARK! *Jaws*! Oh no!"

***

Suddenly, it got very dark. And damp. Their voices began to echo.

Sam's voice was tiny and scared. "Where's Jonah?"

"I don't know," said Scarlett anxiously. "He must have fallen out of the tub when it got so dark in here."

"What should we do?" Sam asked.

"I don't know. I'm scared. Do you know where we are?"

"I think I do. But you're not going to like it," Sam said.

Scarlett shuddered. "I remember the Bible story. I know what you're going to say. We've been swallowed by a whale! That's Jonah's story."

"Not exactly," Sam replied. "We've been swallowed. But not actually by a whale."

"But that's what it says in the Bible!" said Scarlett.

"Not exactly," said Sam, "The Bible says that Jonah was swallowed by a 'a big fish.' It couldn't have been a whale because whales big enough to swallow human beings actually feed on plankton.

They're not meat eaters. Jonah's fish was probably a kind of shark!"

"Then how come we weren't chewed to shreds?"

"It was a very big shark," said Sam.

Scarlett scoffed. "No shark's big enough to swallow three people and a tub without chewing them up."

Sam disagreed. "No shark today, maybe. But in prehistoric times there were kinds of sharks that could do it. I saw them in an exhibit at the natural history museum. Scientists say there were once sharks called megalodons that could grow to be more than fifty feet long. That's as long as a semi!"

"But they're extinct, right?" Scarlett asked.

Sam paused. "Well . . ."

"Do you mean to say that we've been swallowed by . . . a giant prehistoric shark?!"

"That seems to be the case," said Sam.

"We need to find Jonah. Fast!" Scarlett said.

"How will that help?" asked Sam.

"He's going to Nineveh, just as God told him to, whether he wants to or not," said Scarlett. "That's the only way we'll ever get out of this mess."

***

Sam stepped out of the tub carefully, as if he were stepping into a hot bath. But it was more like putting his feet into a pool filled with warm soup. It was too dark to see anything, which was probably just as well. Then Scarlett cautiously stepped out of the tub, her toes stepping on icky, squishy things. One wrapped a tentacle around her ankle. Scarlett shrieked. She tried to kick the thing off. She slipped on something gooey, lost her balance, and fell backward into the soupy liquid.

Sam, trying to catch her, went down too.

They came up sputtering.

"Yuck! Ick!" they both yelled.

"This is disgusting!" Scarlett shouted. "This goop stinks, and it's all over me! How do we get out of here?"

Sam wrinkled his nose at the smell. "I don't know."

Scarlett began to cry. "We've lost our magic carpet! We can't find Jonah! We're stuck in the stinky gut of some prehistoric monster. We'll dissolve bit by bit like the other slimy things in here."

Her sobs turned to gulps. "I'm scared, Sam. Really scared. Do you think that maybe God has forgotten us?"

"No." Sam stood firm. "We may not understand God's reasons. But God would never forget us. We just have to figure out what God wants us to do."

"I don't know what God wants us to do," said Scarlett. "But I do know what God wants Jonah to do. God wants Jonah to go to Nineveh. And Jonah says he's not going. We'll just need to think of a way to make him."

"That's the answer," said Sam. "We have to get Jonah to agree to go to Nineveh. As soon as he does, we'll get out of here."

"But where's Jonah? How are we going to find him? It's pitch-dark in this place. I can't even see my hand," said Scarlett. "How can we find anything in this dark, yucky mess?"

Sam thought for a moment. "Do you still have your cell phone?"

"What are you going to do? Call 9-1-1? I don't think the signal from the inside of an extinct prehistoric shark is going to go very far."

"I'm not worried about the signal," said Sam. "We need light. We can use the flashlight app if our cell phones still work. We'll have light until the charge runs out. Maybe that will be enough."

"I hope so," said Scarlett.

CHAPTER 8

NINEVEH OR BUST!

Getting soaked in seawater hadn't done their cell phones much good. Sam's was completely dead. Scarlett's still had a small charge. But they didn't expect what the cell phone light showed.

The bacteria in the giant fish's gut were bioluminescent, glowing in the dark. The faint glow from Scarlett's cell phone set off waves of purple, red, and green that rippled and pulsed around them in an intestinal version of the

Northern Lights, providing enough light for Scarlett and Sam to see what was around them.

Orange rings of cartilage formed a half dome above their heads. Pink and green fingerlike projections from the walls waved at them as they sloshed through murky soup up to their knees. The liquid teemed with all kinds of living and partially digested sea creatures: eels, fish, and squid, as well as unsavory lumps of unidentifiable beings.

And the smell! It was a cross between a neglected cat litter box and a full garbage can. And not just any garbage can. An overflowing can of ripe garbage left out on the curb for a week in the middle of summer. Scarlett and Sam tried not to gag at every breath.

And there were noises. Creaks, groans, and snorts, punctuated with bubbling gurgles that released foul-smelling gases.

"This critter needs an antacid tablet," said Scarlett, gasping for breath.

"It would take a cargo container of antacid tablets just to make a dent," Sam said. "Do you see any trace of Jonah?"

"No," Scarlett said. "Do you want to turn around and walk in the other direction?"

"Not especially," said Sam. "We have light here. Who knows if we'd still be able to see if we turned around. If we only had some clue . . ."

"Wait! What's that? Did you hear it?"

"Hear what?" Sam asked.

"There! Just listen."

Sam and Scarlett held their breath, trying to hear what Scarlett had heard through the groans, grumbles, burps, and squishes of the giant fish's belly. Sam had almost given up when he finally heard the sound. It was . . . yes! A voice. And not a happy one. Scarlett and Sam could barely make it out as it gasped a few words.

"*I cry to you from the belly of Sheol. Hear my voice . . .*"

"What's Sheol?" Sam asked Scarlett.

"People in Bible times believed it was this nasty pit where you went after you died."

The voice continued.

"You threw me into the deep, to the middle of the ocean. The water surrounded me. The waves covered me . . ."

Sam and Scarlett followed the voice as it led them along the pulsing walls of the big fish's digestive tract.

"There he is!" Scarlett shouted. Long, fingerlike projections from the shark's innards wrapped around Jonah like tentacles, holding him fast as they pushed him down into the murky soup.

"It's digesting him!" Scarlett shrieked. They ran to Jonah, trying to pull him loose. The long slimy tentacles oozed greenish goo that made it impossible for the twins to get a grip.

"It's no use," Jonah gasped. "I'm finished. Run. Save yourselves . . ."

"Listen, Jonah. We aren't going to abandon you. We need you, and you need us," said Scarlett.

"You can free us all," Sam added. "It's easy. All you have to say is . . ."

". . . I'll go to Nineveh," Scarlett said.

"Never!" said Jonah.

"Okay," Scarlett said. "If that's what you want to do." She began to walk away, winking at Sam.

"Where are you going?" Jonah asked anxiously.

"Well," said Scarlett. "If you won't go to Nineveh, what choice do we have but to walk away? I guess we'll have to figure out another way to get out of here."

"Yeah," Sam agreed. "Good luck, Jonah. Nice knowing you."

***

Scarlett and Sam took a few steps back the way they came. Suddenly they heard a shriek.

"WAIT!"

Scarlett turned around. "Is there something you want to say to us?"

"Don't leave me!" Jonah begged. "I don't want to be fish food!"

"You know we can't help you," said Sam. "Only God can help you. Are you going to step up and do what you're supposed to do?"

"Yes! Yes! I'll do anything!"

"Anything doesn't count," said Scarlett. "There's only one thing that you need to do, and you know what it is"

"Okay, I'll do it!" said Jonah.

"Do what?" asked Sam.

"I'll go to . . ."

"Say it," said Scarlett.

"I'll go to NNNNNN . . ."

"Not good enough," Sam said. "It's all or nothing. C'mon, Jonah! You can do it. Say the words with me. I'll go to . . ."

"NINEVEH!" Jonah shouted the word as if it were being pulled out of his throat by a hook. "YES, I'LL DO WHAT GOD WANTS ME TO DO AND GO TO NINEVEH!"

The long digestive fingers released their grip. The walls of the great fish's stomach began flashing yellow, blue, and orange. The sea of goop around their legs began sloshing back and forth. Scarlett, Sam, and Jonah held onto one another to keep from toppling into the murk. Everything around them began to shudder and shake. They felt themselves being whirled around and around as if they were caught inside a giant blender.

"What's happening?" Jonah yelled.

Scarlett and Sam answered. "Nineveh, here we come!"

CHAPTER 9
WELCOME TO NINEVEH

Sam found himself sitting on the white sand of a warm, tropical lagoon. Colorful fish nibbled at his toes. He splashed water from a large seashell over his head to wash away the goo and stink of the giant fish's digestive system.

"Wow!" he said. "That's what I call projectile vomiting."

"And we were the projectiles," Scarlett added as she washed herself down with another seashell of water. She glanced over her shoulder at the enormous fin making its way toward the horizon. She was already thinking about what to do next. "We'll get ourselves cleaned up. The sun's warm and can dry us off. Then we'll need to figure out where we are."

"You wouldn't happen to have any sunscreen?" Sam asked.

"After what we've been through, sunburn is the least of our worries," Scarlett replied.

"Are you sure we can't stay here awhile? It's really nice having a tropical island all to ourselves."

"I know what you mean," Scarlett said. "I'd like to stay and chill as much as you do, Sam. But we're here for a reason. We're on a mission. We have to get Jonah to Nineveh."

Scarlett suddenly remembered something. She looked around. "Where is Jonah? Did you see him?"

"No," Sam said.

"I haven't seen him since the inside of the fish," Scarlett said. She glanced toward the palm trees at the far end of the beach. "Could he be over there, or . . ." Scarlett stopped. She didn't want to say what suddenly crossed her mind. What if Jonah hadn't managed to get out of the big fish? She and Sam might end up stranded thousands of miles and a couple of thousand years away from where they belonged. Scarlett cupped her hands to her mouth and called as loudly as she could, "JONAH! JONAH! WHERE ARE YOU?"

No answer. Scarlett turned to Sam. "Do you think something happened to him? Sam, what if he didn't get out of the big fish with us?"

"He must have," shrugged Sam. "We read the Book of Jonah every year on Yom Kippur. If Jonah didn't make it out of the shark, we'd be reading another book."

"You're right," said Scarlett, relieved. "So we'd better find him."

"Where should we look?" Sam asked.

"Maybe he landed somewhere in those palm trees. Let's go."

That seemed like a good idea. Scarlett and Sam were as clean as a seawater bath was going to get them. The twins walked along the beach until they came to the grove of palm trees.

"Jonah! Are you in there? Jonah!" they called.

Still no answer. "Let's split up," Scarlett said. "We'll cover more trees that way."

"What if we get lost and can't find each other?"

"We won't get lost. It's a small island. Just keep calling out. As long as we can hear each other, we'll know we're okay."

"Good idea," said Sam. He went left and Scarlett went right, both of them calling, "Jonah . . . Jonah . . . Jonah . . ."

Scarlett heard it first: a tiny, scared voice that seemed to come from overhead.

"I cry to God because of my affliction. You cast

me into the heights, in the midst of the trees. Leaves surrounded me about. Flies and lizards swarmed around me . . ."

Scarlett looked up. There was Jonah, clinging to the trunk of a palm tree like a frightened monkey. "Some prophet!" she grumbled to herself. "If God sent him to Pharaoh instead of Moses, we'd still be in Egypt." But she called up to Jonah, "We're here, Jonah. Come down!"

Jonah stared down, surprised to see her. "How did you get out of the whale?"

"Same way you did," Scarlett said. "Come down now. Sam and I have been looking for you."

"I'm afraid of heights," Jonah said. "What if I let go and break my leg?"

"You're not up that high. You can shimmy down the trunk or just drop. There's nothing underneath but sand," said Scarlett.

Jonah didn't move. He clung to the tree with his eyes clamped shut.

"Okay, here I come!" Jonah finally let go. He landed on the sand. Scarlett grabbed his arm to steady him, then quickly let go.

"Yuck! You smell terrible!" She suddenly remembered that Jonah hadn't bathed in the lagoon the way she and Sam had. Jonah raised his eyes to heaven.

"Thank you, God, for rescuing me!"

That's when Sam showed up. "Yuck! What's that smell?"

"It's Jonah," Scarlett said.

"Jonah needs a bath," Sam answered. Before Jonah could say another word, the twins pulled him to the beach and dunked him in the lagoon. They washed him until they all decided he was as clean as he was going to get.

"That's better," said Scarlett and Sam.

Jonah only muttered, "They that observe the lying vanities forsake their own mercy."

"What's that supposed to mean?" Sam asked.

"It's his way of saying, 'thank you,'" said Scarlett.

"You're welcome," said Sam.

"Don't mention it," said Jonah. "Now what?"

"You tell us," said Sam. "You're the prophet."

"I only speak the words God puts in my mouth," Jonah replied. "As of now, my mouth is empty. God hasn't put any words in it."

"God doesn't just speak with words," said Scarlett. "Sometimes God shows you a sign. Like when Moses came across the burning bush in the desert."

"Or when Jacob wrestled with the angel," said Sam. He turned to Jonah. "Well? Do you see any signs?"

"Sorry," Jonah said with a shrug.

Scarlett sighed. "I have an idea. Why don't we sit down and wait for God to send us a sign or tell us what to do next? Meanwhile, it'll give our clothes a chance to dry."

Sam agreed. "Good idea." The three sat down on the trunk of a fallen palm tree and waited for something to happen.

An hour passed. The sun rose high in the sky. "Anybody getting any signs?" Scarlett asked.

"I'm getting thirsty," said Sam.

"I'm getting sleepy," said Jonah. "Do you mind if I find some shade and have a nap?"

"Go ahead," said Scarlett.

"This isn't getting us anywhere," said Sam after Jonah wandered off.

"We have to be patient," Scarlett answered. "The answer will come. I know it will. I can feel it."

"How?" asked Sam. "We're in the middle of nowhere. What if we're cast up on a desert island where no one ever comes? Or maybe if others do come, they'll be pirates or cannibals. What do we do then? How are we supposed to get to Nineveh? Are we anywhere near Nineveh? Can we walk? Build a raft? What?"

"Just be patient," said Scarlett. "It won't take too long. I can feel it."

"Are you getting a sign?" asked Sam.

"Maybe," Scarlett answered. She wouldn't say more than that. She kept staring out at the ocean. Suddenly she stood up. "I see something."

"Where?" Sam asked, trying to follow her gaze.

"Out there. Just below the horizon at eleven o'clock."

Sam saw it too. A speck of red against the blue ocean. It drew closer until Scarlett and Sam could recognize what it was. A sail! A ship was coming toward the island. Scarlett and Sam began jumping up and down, yelling, trying to get the attention of the people on board.

"Hey! You on the boat! We're here! Can you see us?"

The red speck grew larger as it came closer to shore. Scarlett and Sam saw a long ship built for speed. Forty oars dipped and stroked as one to a drumbeat that carried out far over the water.

"Uh-oh. That doesn't look like the ship we took from Jaffa," Sam said. It certainly did not. This ship had the streamlined look of a warship. The long beak on the prow had been designed to tear open the hull of any vessel that got in its way. The armored men on deck carried swords and spears. Others, dressed in black, stalked up and down between the oarsmen, lashing them with whips to get more speed.

"Maybe we can hide in the palm trees," said Sam. "I don't like the look of these guys."

"Me, neither," said Scarlett.

Before they could hide, Jonah appeared on the sand. He yawned and stretched. "That was a good nap. Just what I needed." He stared out to sea. "What's this? A ship! Our dream has come true! My prayers have been answered! We're saved." He began jumping up and down, waving his hands so the men on board could see him. The ship dropped anchor in the shallows of the lagoon. Four armored men leaped overboard. They all had long, curly beards. The one with the longest beard seemed to be the captain. They began walking toward the beach.

Jonah ran toward the men. He flopped down on his knees, raising his arms toward heaven. "Praise God! We're saved!"

"Don't be so sure," Scarlett whispered to Sam.

The captain held out his hand. "Your documents, please."

Scarlett and Sam stared at each other. "You mean like passports? We don't have anything like that," they said. Scarlett dug around in her pocket. "Here's my school ID card. It's wet, though."

"I have a bus pass," said Sam. "How about a library card?"

The captain turned to Jonah. "What about you?"

"The Lord God is my passport!" Jonah said.

"I see," the captain said. He motioned to the soldiers. They stepped forward and, with a few swift motions, tied Sam's, Scarlett's, and Jonah's hands behind their backs. "Let's go," he said, motioning toward the ship with his chin.

"Hey! Wait a minute! Where are you taking us?" Scarlett and Sam cried while Jonah yelled about fire, brimstone, and the Pit of Sheol.

"You've broken the law," the captain told them. "Strangers must have proper documents before being allowed to enter our country. There is a severe penalty for illegal entry . . . unless our king is merciful and decides to sell you as slaves."

"Wait?" Scarlett yelled. "What king? What country? This is a desert island. There's nothing here but seashells and palm trees."

"Doesn't matter," the captain said. "It's our island. Deserted or not, it belongs to our country."

"What country are we in?" asked Sam.

The captain stroked his beard. "You're in Assyria. We're taking you to our capital. Welcome to Nineveh."

CHAPTER 10
SEISMIC EVENTS

Scarlett, Sam, and Jonah rocked back and forth in the hold of the ship as it made its way up the Tigris River to Nineveh. The knee-deep bilge water sloshed back and forth with each stroke of the oars.

"It stinks worse down here than when we were in the fish," said Sam. The shackles on his wrists made it hard to hold his nose.

"How's Jonah doing?" asked Sam.

"Not good," Scarlett said. "I think he's having a meltdown."

Jonah lay curled up in a corner of the hold, crying and moaning to himself. "I cry to you from the depths, O Lord. Hear my prayer. Answer me . . ."

She turned to Jonah. "Please give it a rest, will you, Jonah? That's not helping."

"Go easy on him, Scarlett," said Sam. "He's scared."

"You think I'm not?" Scarlett shot back. "We're chained up in this stinky hole. And we're going to be sold as slaves or worse when the ship gets to Nineveh."

"Oh, God, why are you doing this to me?" moaned Jonah to himself.

"Because you can handle it."

Scarlett stared at Sam. "Did you say something?"

"No," Sam said. "Did you?"

"That wasn't me. I heard a voice loud and clear.

If it wasn't you . . . and it wasn't Jonah . . ." Scarlett glanced over her shoulder at the huddled, weeping prophet. "That leaves . . ."

"Maybe so," said Sam. "Maybe we're not abandoned. Maybe we've all been given a challenge and we just need to figure out how to meet it."

They sat silent for a long time in the smelly hold of the rocking ship. Scarlett spoke first.

"I just remembered something that Grandma Mina told me. She told me about the time when she was going to school at the university, still living in Tehran, and she was arrested by the *Shah*'s police. She said to me, 'Scarlett, you must never let such people know you are scared. Even when they threatened me with all kinds of terrible things, I just laughed in their faces and said, "Do what you like with me. I am just one. There are thousands— tens of thousands—just like me. You can't beat us all. We will never give up."'"

"What does that have to do with us?" Sam

asked. "We're going to Nineveh, not Tehran."

"Don't you get it?" Scarlett said. "We need to be brave and tough like Grandma Mina. We can't let bullies like the captain and his soldiers scare us. And why should we be scared? They may have all the power of Assyria behind them. But you know who we have watching our backs!"

"Who?" said Sam.

"The Big Boss!" said Scarlett. She started swinging her chains against the side of the ship. "Help me, Sam," she said. "Let's make plenty of noise!"

They called on Jonah to help them, but he was too upset, worried that perhaps he'd made a mistake in coming to Nineveh after all.

"Never mind," Scarlett said. "We'll make enough racket for the three of us." They banged away on the ship's hull until the wood started splintering. Blinding light struck their eyes as the hatch above opened.

"Hey! Pipe down! What do you think you're doing?" a sailor yelled.

"We want to see the captain. We demand to speak to him."

The sailor laughed. "Since when do prisoners demand anything?"

"Since right now!" Scarlett said in a loud, brave voice. "Bring your captain to us, or this ship will never reach port. Did you hear me? Bring him NOW!"

"What are you talking about?" Sam whispered. "We're locked in chains. We don't have the power to do anything."

"You and I know that," said Scarlett. "But the captain and his sailors don't."

"Okay! I'm with you," Sam said.

The hatch slammed shut. Scarlett and Sam heard footsteps running back and forth on the deck above their heads. The hatch opened. The captain's angry face glowered down at them.

"How dare you waste my time! What do you want?"

"We are done listening to you. You see our friend Jonah over here?" said Scarlett in a demanding voice, pointing to Jonah. "You will soon be on your knees, begging him for your life. He's a prophet, sent by God to Nineveh with a warning for the people of Assyria. You don't know it yet, but you Assyrians are in big trouble. Big, big trouble!"

"What kind of trouble?" the captain asked. He began to sound nervous.

"We don't talk to the likes of you. Our message is for the king alone. We demand to speak to the king as soon as we reach Nineveh!"

The captain held a quick consultation with two of the ship's officers. Then he turned and left. Soon a sailor came down into the hold and removed the shackles from Scarlett, Sam, and Jonah, inviting them to climb up from the hold into the sunlight.

"Can I get you food or something to drink?" the sailor asked. He looked frightened.

Scarlett didn't mince words. "Yes," she said haughtily. "Also bring us soap, water, and towels so we can wash."

"Aye, aye, Miss!" The sailor ran down to the galley and came back with a tray of pita bread, hummus, dates, goat cheese, and grapes, and wooden cups and a clay jug filled with some kind of fruit juice. Scarlett and Sam helped themselves. But Jonah knelt on the deck, raising his arms to the sky and crying out in a loud voice, "Lord, hear my prayer! Smite the evildoers with the full fury of your wrath! Burn them with everlasting fire . . ."

"Okay, that's enough of that, Jonah," Scarlett called to him. "Want some cheese?"

"Never!" Jonah shrieked. "The food of wicked Nineveh will never pass my lips."

"Suit yourself," said Scarlett. She and Sam

finished their snack. Looking upriver, they saw the walls and towers of Nineveh coming into view as the ship made its way into port. It looked surprisingly shabby for a city that was supposed to be the capital of a world empire. The twins got a closer view as the ship docked.

The whole city seemed to be under repair. Piles of bricks lay in the alleyways and in every vacant lot. Heaps of rubble were all around. Construction scaffolding surrounded the buildings. Their façades, once decorated with colorful tiles, were cracked and bare where the tiles had fallen off.

Scarlett and Sam saw soldiers everywhere. Whoever wasn't a soldier appeared to be a slave. Screams and shouts filled the air, as slaves scurried up and down the scaffolding with bricks, plaster, and mortar to repair the buildings.

"Jonah wasn't kidding," Sam gasped. "Nineveh has to be the worst place on earth."

"You know," said Scarlett thoughtfully, "All this rubble reminds me of earthquakes."

Sam thought for a moment. "They do sort of look like videos from California after an earthquake."

"That's what I was thinking," Scarlett said. "Maybe Nineveh is an area that gets earthquakes. The land is pretty flat. Maybe this city is built on a floodplain. We learned about that in school. Fertile soil is like Jell-O. The soil grows great crops, but it magnifies earthquakes."

"I get it," said Sam. "These guys must be living with constant tremors in this city. And they don't know what causes them. No wonder they're so nasty. Imagine having to constantly wonder if your house is going to fall on top of you while you're sleeping."

Scarlett agreed. "This is good to know."

"Why?" asked Sam.

Scarlett winked at him. "You'll see."

The captain stood on deck talking to a tall man with a beard even longer than his. Its elaborate curls hung below his waist. He wore a conical hat on his head that made him seem even taller.

Scarlett didn't waste any time. She grabbed the captain by the arm. "Listen," she said. "We don't have all day. When are we going to speak to the king?"

The tall man's jaw nearly dropped. "How dare you?"

"How dare I?" said Scarlett. "Do you know who you're talking to?"

"Do you know who *you're* talking to?" the man said. He grew so angry that his face turned the color of a ripe tomato. "I am Adad-Nirari-Shamshad-Ashur-Dan! Uncle to his majesty, King Tukulti-Ninurta the Second."

"Cool!" said Sam. "Good to meet you, Adi. Now stop wasting our time and take us to the king. We must talk to him right away."

"What? I never heard such impudence from slaves!" The king's uncle flew into a rage. "Arrest them!" he shouted. Soldiers came running forward with drawn swords.

"Lord, do not forsake me!" Jonah wailed.

Sam and Scarlett put their arms around Jonah. "Don't you dare!" Scarlett said to the soldiers. "Put those swords away. You see our friend here? His name is Jonah. He's a prophet. He came to Nineveh to warn you of the destruction heading your way if you do not repent your wicked ways."

"That's right," said Sam. "Unless the king hears Jonah's message, Nineveh is doomed."

"D-O-O-M-E-D!" Scarlett shouted. "That's DOOMED with a capital *D*."

The soldiers stopped in their tracks. Even the king's uncle looked apprehensive.

Scarlett turned to Jonah. "Go ahead. Tell them, Jonah. Tell them what God sent you here to say."

"Go on," said Sam. "Now's your chance. Let 'em have it."

Jonah faced the Assyrians. His mouth opened and shut, but no sound came out. He tried again. This time, he only got as far as, "G-G-G-G-G . . ."

The Assyrians began laughing. "Some prophet!"

"Enough of that," said the king's uncle. "You've wasted my time, and you will be punished."

"Don't you dare!" said Scarlett. "If you lay one hand on us . . ." She stopped. Then what?

Sam jumped in. "This city will be destroyed. Nothing will be left of it, not even a candy wrapper. When God gets finished with Nineveh, you will be sorry you didn't wait to hear what Jonah has to say."

Scarlett followed Sam's lead. "Not one brick will be left standing in this city. Not even a lizard will be left alive."

That's when Jonah joined in. Suddenly the full power of prophecy poured from his mouth. "Woe to you, Nineveh! Woe to you, Assyria! The fires of Sheol will consume you! Demons will feast on your bones!"

"That's really good," Scarlett whispered, admiringly. She faced the Assyrians. "Did you hear that? The prophet has spoken. We demand to meet your king. We're done waiting. You have ten seconds. Countdown starting now: ten . . . nine . . . eight . . ." She counted off the seconds on her fingers.

Sam continued. "Seven . . . six . . ."

"Five . . . four . . . three . . ." said Jonah.

"They're bluffing," the king's uncle said. "Arrest them. Now!"

The soldiers came forward with their swords raised. Jonah pointed across the dock at the tallest tower on the waterfront. "Behold, sinners of Assyria! The Hand of the Lord descends on Nineveh!"

"The tower! It's moving!" Scarlett gasped.

Within seconds, everything was moving. A noise like a hundred freight trains ripped through the air. The ship rocked back and forth. Everyone on board ran to grab hold of something to keep from being knocked over. Waves from the river crashed over the wharfs, lifting up entire ships and smashing them into buildings. Cracks rippled through the city walls. Scarlett and Sam heard screams as a tower overlooking the port came crashing down. Then it stopped.

"You were right," whispered Sam. "Seismic tremors."

"Yup, earthquake," said Scarlett. "My hunch was right." She turned to the king's uncle. "How'd you like that? That was just a taste. Want more?"

The king's uncle threw himself down at Jonah's feet. "No! Have mercy! Do not destroy our city! I will escort you to the king at once."

"Good," said Scarlett.

"Uh, we don't like to walk," said Sam.

"I will arrange to have you carried to the palace by a chariot."

"See that you do," said Scarlett.

Jonah looked around. A smile of grim satisfaction crossed his face. He had faced the dreaded Assyrians, and they had trembled. Soon they would face Heaven's wrath. He had no doubt of that.

CHAPTER 11
DANGER ZONE

Slaves had begun clearing away the rubble in the streets by the time a golden chariot inlaid with precious gems arrived. Two powerful horses pulled it through the streets. No one waved or cheered. Everyone kept on working, looking serious and frightened.

"How come everybody seems so scared?" Scarlett asked the driver. "In our town people love to stand in the streets and cheer when something like a parade comes by."

The driver shook his head. "Why should we look happy? What is there to cheer about here in Nineveh? We're all slaves. We'll never see our homes and families again."

Scarlett and Sam felt sad hearing that. Jonah just stared at the ruined buildings.

The chariot dropped them off at the palace gates. Platoons of soldiers armed with swords and spears paraded back and forth. Each one had a long, curly beard. Even the carvings on the walls depicted gods and kings with beards. Scarlett and Sam saw other carvings of winged bulls with human heads. Even the bulls had beards!

"They must go for beards here," Scarlett whispered to Sam. All the men they'd seen so far had similar long, curly beards. "Do you think the beards are all real?"

"Probably not," Sam whispered back. "Do you think I'd look good with a beard?"

"Not one of those," said Scarlett. "It'd look like some large, furry animal attached itself to your face."

But they didn't have time to think any more about that. The soldiers at the palace entrance challenged them.

"State your business!"

"We've come to see the king!" Scarlett said in a loud voice.

"The king's uncle has arranged it. Now lead us to your king!" Sam added. The soldiers stepped forward threateningly, but suddenly a voice called from inside the palace.

"Let them through!" A man who looked like some sort of official, because his beard was longer and curlier than the rest, helped Scarlett and Sam off the chariot. He ushered them through the rows of soldiers to the throne room.

"When are we going to see the king?" Sam demanded.

"Right now," the official said. "But I am warning you. Don't waste the king's time. Say what you have to say and be done."

Jonah said nothing as Scarlett and Sam reached for his hands. Suddenly he stretched his arms wide and shouted out the familiar Hebrew words, *"Sh'ma Yisrael, Adonai Eloheynu, Adonai Ekhad! Hear, O Israel. The Lord, Our God, The Lord is One."*

"That's the Sh'ma," said Sam.

"You got it, Jonah! That's telling them!" Scarlett said.

Scarlett, Sam, and Jonah locked arms. They strode down the corridor filled with soldiers until they came to an enormous room. It, too, was filled with soldiers with even longer beards. Standing among the soldiers were groups of men and women in different costumes.

"Those must be ambassadors from other countries," Sam whispered. "They look a little nervous."

"So would we. But we have something they don't," said Scarlett.

"What?" Sam asked.

Jonah answered. "The Big Boss!"

"That's right," said Scarlett. "No fear!"

"No fear!" said Sam.

"No fear!" said Jonah.

***

Moments later, Scarlett, Sam, and Jonah found themselves standing before the throne of the king of Assyria, the most powerful and feared ruler of the ancient world.

The throne, made entirely of gold, looked like an escalator at a mall. Fifty steps led up to the seat at the top. A pair of animals—also made of gold—stood on the sides of each step: lions, bears, tigers, elephants, camels, giraffes, leopards, eagles, gazelles, bulls, sheep, goats, and chickens.

"Looks like they were running out of animals toward the end," Scarlett whispered to Sam.

She didn't have time to say more. A blast of trumpets sounded. More soldiers came marching in, escorting the king to the throne. The king, a tiny person with a curly beard that went down to his knees, stopped before the first step. The two lions, roaring mechanical roars, lifted him up to the next step. Then the mechanical bears took over, followed by the mechanical tigers, elephants, camels, etc. By the time the king reached his throne, the top of his crown was only a few inches from the ceiling. The king sat down. With a satisfied smile, he glanced over the crowds gathered far below him.

Scarlett nudged Sam with her elbow. She tried not to giggle. "That's the king of Assyria, the guy the whole world fears? Don't you think all this hoopla is a little silly?"

"Do you think the beard's real?" Sam asked.

"I don't know," Scarlett replied.

"Silence!" the king commanded. He had a high, screechy voice. He glared down at Scarlett, Sam, and Jonah. "Nobody speaks unless I speak to them. Do you understand? Now, before we go any further, the three of you must bow to me. Show them how it's done!" he ordered those around him.

Everyone in the room dropped to their knees and groveled facedown on the floor. Everyone, that is, except for Scarlett, Sam, and Jonah.

"I'm waiting," the king said.

"You'll have to keep waiting," said Scarlett.

"You won't bow to me?" the king yelled.

"Tell him, Jonah," said Scarlett.

Jonah stuck out his chin. He folded his arms across his chest. "We bow only to God."

"Oh, yeah?" said the king. "And which god is that? Osiris of Egypt? Bel Marduk of Babylon? Ishtar of Phoenicia? There are many gods. And you know what? I conquered them all! I burned their temples. I looted their treasure houses.

I marched their priests off as slaves. Do you know what else? Those great and powerful gods didn't lift a finger to stop me. Want to know why? Because the only god is Ashur, the God of Assyria! The All-Powerful God of Nineveh!"

Everybody groveling on the floor answered with one voice, "Hail to Ashur the All-Powerful."

The king continued. "Go on. Tell me the name of your god. I'll swat him like a fly!"

"Did you hear what he said?" Scarlett hissed at Jonah. "Nobody talks about God like that. Set him straight, Jonah. Go on! Tell him."

Jonah pointed his finger at the king. "Listen to me! I have a message for you. There is only one God, the God who is the creator of the world. God rules the universe. The One and Only True God is . . ." Jonah paused to let the words sink in. "The God of Israel!"

"Israel?" The king burst out laughing. So did everyone else in the throne room. Not only did they laugh; they rolled around the floor with glee as if they had just heard the funniest joke in the world.

"Did you hear that?" the king said. "The God of Israel!" Which made everyone laugh even harder.

"I don't get it," Sam said to Scarlett. "What's so funny?" Jonah looked as if he were about to explode with fury. The king continued.

"My grandfather Sennacherib crushed Israel like a bug! Those Israelites thought they could stand against Assyria. Grandpa burned their capital city Samaria to the ground. He left nothing but rubble. A few more years and people won't even remember that a city once stood there. He marched the people off as slaves—all the ten tribes of Israel. He dispersed them so far away that they'll never come back. No one will ever hear from them again. The God of Israel? Where was that God when all of this was happening? Your precious God hid like a mouse when our Great God Ashur stomped across his land!"

Scarlett heard someone sniffle. She looked at

Jonah. He was crying. "It's true," he murmured.

"No, it's not!" said Scarlett. She walked up to the first step of the throne. The mechanical animals started growling at her. "Quiet!" she yelled. The menagerie fell silent. She looked up at the king. "I don't know why God turned away from Israel then. I do know it wasn't because God was afraid."

"That's true. God was never afraid," said Jonah quietly to Sam, dabbing at his eyes.

"Then why don't you say something? You're a prophet. C'mon! What are you waiting for?"

Jonah squared his shoulders. He marched to the foot of the throne. Standing next to Scarlett, he looked up at the king.

"There is only one God, the God of Israel. Get ready to behold God's power."

The people in the throne room began to mill about in confusion. Even the king looked nervous. Everyone waited. Five minutes. Ten minutes. Nothing happened.

Scarlett jumped in. "That's right!" she shouted. "Behold God's power." She looked at Jonah. Jonah shook his head.

"Not yet," said Jonah.

The king started laughing. "I'm waiting."

"You're a prophet. Do something!" Sam hissed desperately at Jonah.

"I will. Be patient. Ten . . . nine . . . eight . . ."

"Enough of this nonsense. Take them away," said the king.

". . . three . . . two . . . one . . ."

The soldiers drew their swords. Suddenly Jonah roared, "NOW!"

The palace began to shake. The pillars holding up the room began tottering. The king's throne wobbled, then collapsed, pitching him headfirst into the mob of people struggling to reach the exits. The ceiling crashed down on the throne, smashing it to bits. The mechanical rooster gave out a faint *cock-a-doodle-doo*. Then all was silent.

"What's going on?" Sam called to Scarlett.

"Aftershocks," she yelled back. Jonah stared around, amazed. Then he grinned.

"Behold the Power of the Lord!"

Within minutes, more soldiers poured into the throne room. They plucked the king from the wreckage of his throne and gave him some dire news.

"Your Majesty, our city is doomed. The Temple of Ashur has collapsed. Nothing is left. Our great god is a pile of broken stone!"

"And your uncle is no more. He was worshipping before the god when Ashur fell on top of him."

The king screamed. He pulled off his fake beard, revealing himself to be just a boy, and cried, "What will become of me? What will become of my kingdom? My uncle is gone! Who will tell me what to do? O Great God of Israel, have mercy on us!" He fell at Jonah's feet, weeping as he clutched Jonah's ankles.

Scarlett and Sam stared in surprise. "The king! He's just a kid!"

It was true. Without the crown, the false beard, the mechanical throne, and the armies of marching soldiers, the king of Assyria was just a boy. He could have been one of Scarlett and Sam's friends from school.

"Don't hurt me!" the king pleaded.

"We won't hurt you," Scarlett said. "You're a kid like us. Why are you acting like such a brat?"

"It's not my fault. My uncle made me do it. He said I have to be mean and cruel or nobody will listen to me. He said I have to beat slaves and chop off heads. Otherwise, nobody will love and respect me."

"Your uncle is wrong. Being cruel isn't the way to go. People don't respect you when you behave like that. They're just scared of you," said Scarlett. "Fear isn't respect."

"And it sure isn't love," Sam added.

"I didn't know what else to do," the king said in tears. "The kings of Assyria have always been like that. My dad was cruel. So was his father. And his father before him."

"So what? You don't have to be like them. What if we show you another way?" said Scarlett. "Our friend Jonah is a prophet. He's been sent to Nineveh with an important message that you need to hear. Go on, Jonah. Tell the king what he needs to do."

Jonah spoke. "Listen, O King! I will tell you how God smote Egypt in the days of Moses. Thus were the Egyptians punished for their countless sins with the Ten Plagues of Egypt." And Jonah began to recite the Ten Plagues in ancient Hebrew.

"What's Jonah saying?" asked Sam.

Scarlett listened. Her eyes opened wide. "He's reciting the Ten Plagues—in Hebrew!"

"Why?" said Sam. "It's not Passover. We're not

at the seder. The Assyrians don't speak Hebrew. Look at them. They don't understand what Jonah's talking about."

Scarlett suddenly realized what Jonah was doing. "I've got it, Sam. Jonah is doing what God has commanded him to do, warning the Assyrians to change their ways. But he doesn't think God is being fair, so he's not really delivering God's message. He's preaching to them all right . . . but in a language they don't understand. They won't know what he's saying. If they don't understand what he's telling them, they can't change their ways and be saved by God."

"That's not the right thing to do," said Sam. "How can we help?"

"We can't let Jonah get away with it. The Assyrians deserve a chance to become better people. That's what God wants. That's why God has sent Jonah to Nineveh."

"Do you think that's why God sent us here too?"

"Maybe, Sam. God does what God does. God commanded Jonah to preach. God didn't say we couldn't preach too. Shall we give it a try?"

Sam grinned. "Let's do it!"

"What's he saying?" the king asked Sam and Scarlett, staring at Jonah who was shouting, waving his arms, stomping his feet, and carrying on.

"We'll translate for you," Sam said. "He's saying that everything that happens comes from God. God sent us here with a warning for you because God loves the people of Nineveh."

"As unlovable as you are," Scarlett added.

Sam continued. "God could destroy you in a moment, as you saw. No one would be sorry about that because the rest of the world knows you behave badly. You've built your kingdom on violence and cruelty. Many people wouldn't shed a tear if God erased your city the way you've erased so many others."

The king began weeping. "I'm sorry."

"We know. And we truly believe that deep down inside you have a kind heart. But 'I'm sorry' isn't enough," said Scarlett. "You have to change your ways."

"How?" the king asked.

"For starters, free all the slaves of Assyria. Nothing is as wrong as slavery."

Sam joined in. "End all your wars. Call back your armies."

"You've heard God's word from the Prophet Jonah," said Scarlett. "From now on, live in peace with everyone. If you do, God won't give Nineveh the punishment it deserves. Lions can lie down with lambs, and everyone can live under their own vine and fig tree. Isn't that better than what you have now? Slavery, cruelty, violence, fear, and the trembling of the earth under your feet?"

"You're right," the king said. "Why didn't I realize this before? Why did I let my cruel uncle bully me? All praise to the God of Israel for giving us a second chance! We'll change our ways. We'll start today. We'll start right now."

"Yeah!" said Sam.

"Hooray! You're awesome!" said Scarlett, giving the king a hug. Everybody cheered for this new chapter for Nineveh.

CHAPTER 12
THE GOURD

One could accuse the Assyrians of many things, except one. No one could say the Assyrians were not thorough. When they destroyed a country, not even a grasshopper was left alive. When they looted a city, they left nothing behind—not even a nail. And when they repented, they did it completely.

Once the king gave the order, his people set about changing their ways. They tore their clothes to apologize for their evil ways. They dressed in rags. They heaped dust and ashes on their heads. Whole families, from the highest nobles to the poorest beggars, weeped and moaned, beseeching forgiveness from those they'd wronged.

Most astonished were the slaves. Their masters now groveled at their feet, kissing their toes, wailing, "I'm so sorry! Please forgive me!"

"That's a good start," Scarlett told the king, who was banging his head on the palace steps in sorrow at his own bad behavior. "But it's not enough."

"You can't just be sorry," said Sam. "If you've done wrong, you have to make it right."

"Gotcha! That's Phase II," the king said. "I'm already working on it."

Indeed he was. The king pressed the royal seal into a clay tablet. He ended the wars, called home the armies, and freed the slaves. He didn't stop there. He ordered his soldiers and sailors to help the former slaves get back to their homes and families. Fleets of ships and camel caravans were soon traveling to the war-ravaged lands. The treasure they carried would help the slaves rebuild their countries.

Unfortunately for the prisoners who had been carried off from Israel, they had been sent so far away that no one any longer remembered where they were. The records had been lost, so the Israelites remain lost to this day, and have become known as the Ten Lost Tribes of Israel.

Freeing the slaves had an unforeseen benefit to Assyria. The fleets and caravans didn't return to Nineveh empty. They carried cargoes of valuable goods back from their travels: wine, spices, incense, textiles, and pottery. And since the wars were ended, traders from distant lands no longer feared coming to Nineveh.

Some of the former slaves even decided they liked living in Nineveh. They started their own businesses, buying and selling. Trade of all kinds flourished.

Since the king no longer had to pay for wars and armies, the kingdom prospered. Money poured into the treasury, allowing the king to do even more to help his people.

The king set about rebuilding the city. He built schools, hospitals, and libraries.

"Doing good certainly does pay!" the king exclaimed, looking over his gleaming new city filled with happy people. "I'm so glad you came to Nineveh. I apologize for being nasty in the beginning. I owe you two big time. What can I do for you?"

"Just get us tickets on the next caravan leaving for Jaffa," Sam said.

"Consider it done," the king said. "One leaves tomorrow."

A thought suddenly crossed Scarlett's mind. "Sam, have you seen Jonah?"

"No," Sam said. "I wonder where he went."

"I'll send out a search party," the king said.

"That's okay, we'll find him," Scarlett and Sam said, as they set out to look for the prophet.

***

"Have you seen a strange-looking dude walking around, mumbling to himself?" they asked people. A group of workers repairing the street pointed to a hill overlooking the city. "We saw a guy like that heading up there an hour ago."

"Thanks!" said Scarlett and Sam. They started up the hill.

***

It was a steep climb. Scarlett and Sam were both out of breath by the time they reached the top. They looked around. "There he is!" cried Sam.

Jonah sat on the ground underneath a trellis holding the withered remains of a dried-up plant. He was moaning. From time to time he yelled out, "Why have You forsaken me? Why did you break Your promise?"

"Who's he talking to?" Scarlett said.

Sam rolled his eyes. "He was always a little unusual."

"Let's tell him to get a move on," said Scarlett. "We don't want to miss the Jaffa caravan. It might be the last one leaving for a month."

***

As Scarlett and Sam came closer, they saw that Jonah was sitting on a carpet that looked an awful lot like Grandma Mina's!

Sam nudged Scarlett. "Do you see what I see? Maybe we don't have to go to Jaffa after all."

"Maybe not. But we still have to get Jonah

home," Scarlett said. She approached him. "Jonah?"

He turned around, surprised to see the twins.

"What are you doing up here?" Scarlett asked him.

"I came to weep," Jonah said.

"About what?" said Sam. "Everything's going great. There are no more wars. The slaves are free. Nineveh's turned into a happy place to live. What is there to cry about?"

Jonah wiped his nose on his sleeve. "My gourd died."

"Your what?" said Sam.

"My gourd!" Jonah pointed to the withered plant on the trellis. "I sat down under the trellis, hoping to get a little shade. Suddenly a plant started to grow next to me. I've never seen a plant grow so fast. It burst out of the ground. Its leaves covered the trellis, giving me shade. I thanked God for the gourd. Suddenly an east wind came blowing out of the desert. The gourd dried up. Worms started eating it. It died before my eyes, leaving me with nothing but the sun beating on my head. And the citizens of Nineveh are unpunished."

Scarlett was angry. "So you think God should have destroyed the city? You think those people deserved to be destroyed? What about the slaves who were living there? What about the kids? The babies? There are animals in Nineveh too. Doggies, kitties, camels, goats, horses. What did they ever do wrong? Don't you think God cares about the city and those who live there? God created them!"

"I guess so. But God should be fair. The wicked should be punished, but you're right—the slaves and the children and the doggies, kitties and other animals didn't do anything wrong. Oh, what a world!" shouted Jonah as he ran off with Grandma Mina's carpet.

Sam watched as Jonah disappeared down the hillside. "Should we try to catch Jonah and bring him back? What if we miss the caravan to Jaffa? What about our carpet?"

"Maybe we should try to get to Jaffa without Jonah or the carpet," said Scarlett.

Suddenly the mountain, the trellis, the city, and the dried-up gourd began swirling 'round and 'round.

"Something's happening! Hold on, Sam! Here we go!" Scarlett yelled.

CHAPTER 13

HOME FREE

The twins found themselves stumbling through the door of Dihanian's carpet shop. Scarlett was the first to catch her breath.

"I'm so sorry, Mr. Dihanian. I don't know what we're going to tell Grandma Mina."

"We looked everywhere for that driver. We nearly got run over by a bus," said Sam. "What do you think we should do? Maybe we can call Loft and see if they can track down the driver.

He might not even know that the carpet's still in his car."

"Carpet?" said Mr. Dihanian. "You mean this one?" He reached behind the desk and pulled out Grandma Mina's carpet.

"Huh?" said Scarlett and Sam. "How did you find it?"

"I didn't find it. It found me," Mr. Dihanian said. "I'll get it back to your grandmother. Your Loft driver brought it back while you were out looking for him. He discovered it in his car after he dropped you off. I asked if he wanted to wait for you. He said no; he was in a hurry. He left a message."

Mr. Dihanian handed Sam a folded piece of paper. Scarlett and Sam read it together.

Dear Scarlett and Sam,

I'm sorry I was such a pain on our adventure, especially after we got to Nineveh. Now that I've had time to think about it, I realize that you two taught me a lot. I'm going to try to be a better person from now on. I've been hanging out with the king. We play chess every evening. He's really a nice kid. This may surprise you, but I've decided to stay in Nineveh. It's a nice place once you know your way around. I'm glad that God gave Nineveh and the king a second chance after all.

I'm glad I could get your carpet back to you. I know how worried you were about losing it. I hope we'll get to see each other again. Look me up if you ever get to Nineveh. Apartment 7, Red House, Street of the Dragon.

Your friend,
Jon

"Gosh!" Sam exclaimed after reading the note. "Do you think we'll ever see Jonah again?"

"Not if I can help it," said Scarlett as they headed for the bus stop.

About the Author

Eric A. Kimmel has been writing for children for over forty years. His more than one hundred titles include such classics as *Anansi and the Moss-Covered Rock*, *Gabriel's Horn*, and *Hershel and the Hanukkah Goblins*. He lives in Portland, Oregon.

About the Illustrator

Ivica Stevanovic has illustrated numerous picture books, as well as book covers and graphic novels. He lives in Veternik, Serbia, with his wife, who is also a children's illustrator, and their daughter.

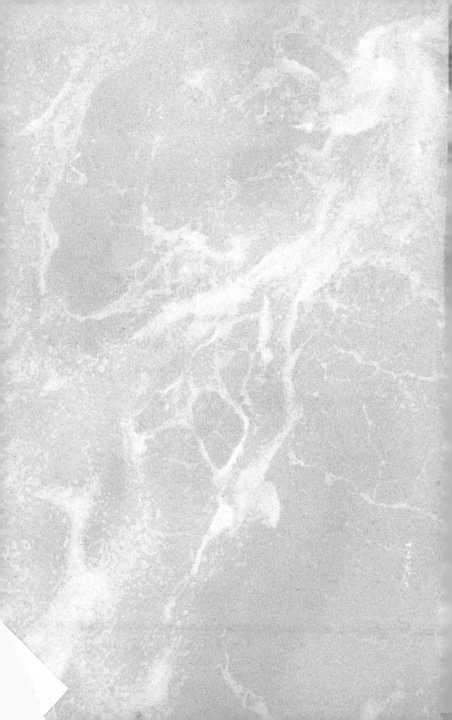